Farm Ani

Characters

Red Group

Blue Group

Purple Group

All

Setting A farm

My Picture Words

cow

duck

horse

pig

My Sight Words

a

am

eat

I

who

I eat grass.

Who am I?

I am a 

!

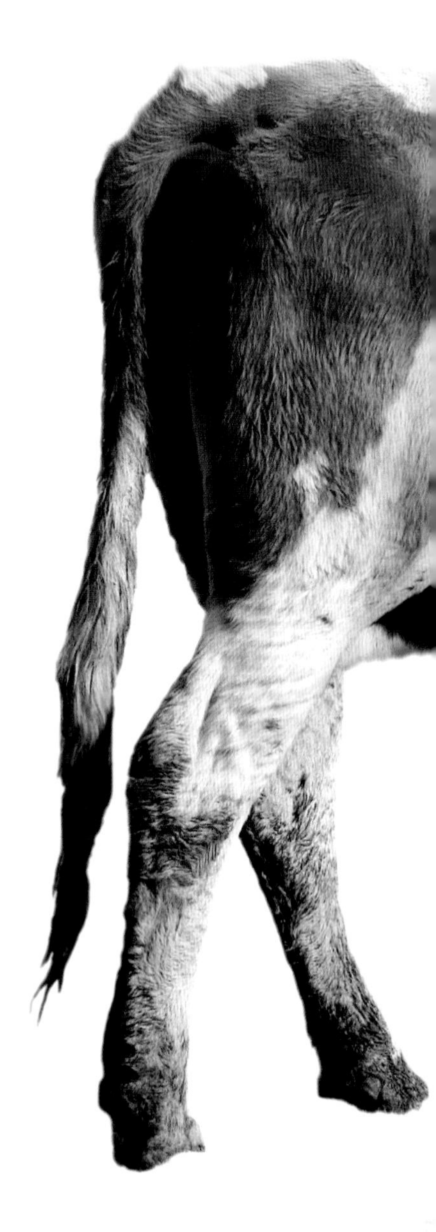

I eat  .

corn

Who am I?

I am a  !

pig

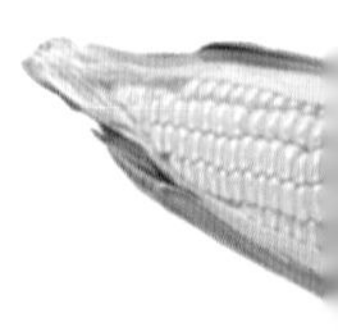

I eat  .

Who am I?

I am a  !

I eat  .

Who am I?

I am a  !

Who am I?

The End